UNMASKING THE
PAIN Within

One Woman's Journey through Deceit, Manipulation, & Marital Abuse

PATTY McCALL

Cover Design by D. Tucker

Co-Editorial by Lisa Ann Vombrack

Photography by Rachel Sudduth, J Squared Photography, and Chad Peters.

Unmasking the Pain Within
One Woman's Journey through Deceit, Manipulation, & Marital Abuse
ISBN: 0-88144-342-5
Copyright © 2008 by Patty McCall

Published by
Yorkshire Publishing Group
7707 East 111th Street South, Suite 104
Tulsa, Oklahoma 74133
www.yorkshirepublishing.com

Dedication

This book is dedicated to all of the following people. I want to thank each and every one of them for being my friends and for supporting and helping me through all the difficult times.

Irene Clark (Mom)

Sherry Patterson

Lori Lenhart

Rachel Sudduth

Kim Barnell

Barbie Davis

Janet Kaufman

Jody French

Terri Breedlove

Julie Smith

Joann Overfelt

Tiffany Overfelt

Carmen Bentoncourt

Dave Freer

Judea Cavoto

Acknowledgements

Many thanks to Lisa Ann Vombrack for blessing me with her friendship and for her encouragement in helping this book become a reality. Over the last several years, our friendship has deepened as we both came to realize that we shared many similar experiences. As a result, we have come to experience a deep, heartfelt spiritual connection with each other which I hope is reflected in this book.

This journey began while we were both working together as film producers. I mentioned my story to Lisa, sharing with her that I needed help in putting my story in manuscript form. She was both receptive and excited to help me on this project, and as a result it went from my handwritten notes to the actual finished book which you now hold in your hands.

During this creative process, our collaborative efforts led us to dream a little bigger than just getting the story published. We are both very passionate about helping other women gain the victory over abusive relationships. As soon as this book is complete, we plan to work on a script to get this true story out to as many women as possible.

Table of Contents

Introduction

This book is one woman's life story — my story — and describes how I overcame many obstacles: pain, abuse, fear, and the numerous challenges I encountered in my life. It started out simply as my attempt to pass on to my daughters my life story, motivated by the fact that I did not want them to experience the same trauma and abuse I had endured during my life. I wanted them and other young women to see what a real problem abuse is in so many relationships and how women are ashamed to talk about it when they are going through it. My goal was to give them the tools to help them cope during an abusive situation and to give them hope and support afterwards as they recover and move on with their lives.

My desire in writing this is that through the scriptures and my one-on-one relationship with God, I can help others deal with their pain. The healing process does take time, but as my story reveals, there is a light at the end of the tunnel.

I pray to be open to God's message of comfort and hope; to hear His voice, and to take every opportunity to be an encouragement to someone who may need me.

CHAPTER ONE

A Chance Meeting

I was headed back to Tulsa, Oklahoma. On my way, I pulled into a 7-11 convenience store in Coweta, driving my new Z-28 Camaro with the T-tops down. As I exited the store, a well-built, dark-haired, hunk yelled in my direction, "Can I drive your car?" I responded with a laugh. Arnold, which I later found out was his name, added, "...of course, that would only be with you in it. I met you a few days ago in a club and you were swing dancing with my friend all evening." I had no recollection of him, but I did remember having lots of fun dancing with his friend. Arnold asked where I was going for the evening. I told him my friend Sherry and I were going to that very same club in Tulsa, Oklahoma to dance again that evening. coincidentally, he was going to the same place, and asked, "Will you dance with me tonight?" "Sure," I replied, totally unaware of how my life was about to change.

About midnight Arnold showed up at the club and we danced, in between his flirtations. Throughout the night he made comments about coming home with me. I wasn't at all interested in that, but I did give him my phone number. The next day he called, asking if he could come over. It turned out to be a very cold, and misty day and all he had was a motor-cycle, which made me feel a little sorry for him. When he came to my door he was shivering like an icicle, so I let him in. We spent the evening watching a movie, and afterward I said he could sleep on the couch as I couldn't see him freezing to death going home that evening.

The next day was Monday, and Arnold headed back on the forty-five minute ride to his home. I went to my job at FNB, a locally owned bank in Muskogee, where I was a supervisor responsible for over twenty tellers. I too had started out as a teller the summer after I finished high school. Mike Leonard, the President of the bank saw my potential and had sent me to classes to further my career in banking, promoting me to supervisor after only a few months of working there. As part of my commitment to work, it was very important to me to come to work completely focused — absolutely no distrac-tions. But to my surprise a dozen long stem red roses arrived on my desk later that afternoon.

With a long day's work ended, I picked up my son Jason from my Mom's at 4:30 and headed home to relax and spend quality time with my son. Not even a half hour after I had gotten home, Arnold was calling me, wanting to come over. I was way too tired and didn't feel like company.

But Arnold's persistent pattern continued, and each day, like clockwork he would call as soon as I would get home. As my schedule was way too busy during the week to see him; we compromised, seeing each other only on the weekends. One Saturday evening we decided to go see a movie. Since I didn't want to ride on his motorcycle, we decided to take my car.

During our conversation he informed me that he worked for a cable company and explained how crazy his schedule was. It was never consistent, he told me; sometimes he had to work ten days in a row. In spite of that, we did continue dating for a couple of months and not too long afterwards he got an offer to go to Houston, Texas for a cable TV job.

So, I went about my life. Arnold remained persistent as ever, however, sometimes calling two to three times a day, leaving messages to see me. After only two weeks had passed, he bought me a plane ticket to fly to Houston, Texas for the weekend. Every other weekend he would fly back to Oklahoma or fly me to Houston, Texas, and this went on for about a year. During this period I was also juggling my time dating another guy, Dennis. Arnold then surprised me by informing me he was coming back to Oklahoma.

CHAPTER TWO

Courting and Marriage

Before Arnold had left for Houston, he had been living with his parents. His Dad had been paralyzed from the neck down, the result of a horse and buggy accident. As a result, his Mom worked running a bar, and Arnold had to take care of his younger sister and brother. Upon his return to Oklahoma, Arnold didn't want to move back in with his parents, so he asked me if he could move into my apartment with me. Without giving it much thought, I reluctantly made the decision to let Arnold move in with me. I had no choice but to tell Dennis I couldn't see him anymore.

At the time, I had a female roommate living with me; a "wild child" bringing home a different guy almost every weekend. Since my son was with me I had to have strict rules

in my home, and I wouldn't allow her to bring anyone home during the week. But she refused to abide by my rules, which gave me no choice but to give her a thirty day notice.

As our relationship developed, my son Jason seemed to really hit it off with Arnold. I usually didn't have men around Jason, but the two of them got along so well and it was now over a year since I had been seeing Arnold. We adjusted well, living together like a family. Arnold seemed like he adored me and would do any thing for me; he wanted to stay in Oklahoma to be close to us. Luckily, he was able to get a job with a local cable station. Since my credit was strong, I decided to apply for a loan for a new house in Ft. Gibson. I wanted to have our own place, in a location where Jason could go to a good school. Fortune was at our back, and we moved into our brand spanking new little twelve hundred square foot house in an adorable neighborhood right behind the school.

After a couple of months Arnold and I talked seriously about having our own child. With talking about babies and such, Arnold asked me to marry him, and I said "yes," wanting to be married before I became pregnant. At the time, we didn't want to spend a lot of money on a wedding, so we went to the Justice of the Peace for our ceremony.

But we did honeymoon in Cancun, Mexico. The beach was breathtaking, with its beautiful white sand and calm, clear, aqua blue water. We had so much fun together; lots of partying, sightseeing, seeing the ruins of the island, and we even went on the glass bottom boat. It was a wonderful place to go for a honeymoon and to start our new life together.

CHAPTER THREE

A Parent's Worst Nightmare

The Pain... *Enduring a loss of a loved one is unbearable... many people have endured this type of **pain***...showing all of us to embrace life to its fullest each and ever day, not knowing when it will be taken away from us...

One horrific day... I remember not being at home all day, out looking for a new car not knowing that my Mom and Dad were desperately trying to get in touch with me. But back then, we didn't have cell phones. I could tell by the kind of messages they had left on the answering machine, that something was very wrong and urgent. When I returned their call my grief-stricken Dad spoke these words, "Your brother was killed by a semi truck. It hit his car head on, killing him instantly."

I could hardly catch my breath, hysterically screaming, *"God, why did you let this happen? He was only eighteen years old?"* But I knew in my heart, that you can't always understand why situations or tragedies happen in life or try to second-guess the Lord. It was then I first learned: Sometimes you just have to **let go...and let God** and hold on to your faith.

Grabbing my things, I immediately rushed over to my parents' house. I ran to my Mom and embraced her, consoling her over the loss of my brother. Still reeling from the shock, we prayed to the Lord for strength and guidance in making all the necessary funeral arrangements.

Three tragic days later... Our family attended my dear younger brother's funeral. Everything was arranged so beautifully, just the way he would have wanted it. After the preacher ended the service my Dad and I walked Mom up to the casket, which was closed because of the trauma of the accident. A picture of my brother's sweet face sat atop the casket. We left Mom there by herself to have her last moment with her son, but when the ushers were ready to take the casket to the graveside she refused to leave. Instead, she stood there in a trance, tears streaming down her anguished face. Dad and I stood on either side of her and gently took her by the arms to walk her out of the church. She collapsed in a heap; so we fanned her ashen face back to consciousness, as we firmly lift her up so we could finally leave for the gravesite. It was until we arrived, that reality hit all of us hard, our faces streaming with tears as we realized we were

never going to be able to see or hold Robby again. I said a prayer of inner peace:

"Be with him, Lord the strength I have is not my own; it comes through faith in you. And though so often I can't see the way, I have the reassurance of your presence in my life, to help me meet the challenge of each day. With Your help, Lord, I can do all things."

At twenty-one I was the older, stronger sister, and the tragedy of my brother's untimely death left me no choice but to help my Mom cope with life on a day-to-day basis. Thank the Lord, my younger sister was only fifteen years old, and still living at home, which did provide comfort to my Mom in spite of my brother's absence. But watching my Mom's pain was killing me. Even now, twenty eight years after that tragedy, my Mom still has a difficult time on my brother's birthday and on the anniversary of Robby's death.

*You **overcome,** give it to the Lord and be strong...*

CHAPTER FOUR

A Year of Firsts

Just as our new family life was about to begin, Arnold lost his local cable TV job. Someone found out that he had been committing fraud by making false receipts and claiming them as part of his expenses. This untimely bad news made me wonder for the first time in our relationship, about his character as a husband, and especially now that he would be a new father to my child. With the baby coming soon, I hoped he was going to look for another job. Apparently, he had different intentions.

When I got involved with Arnold, I had no idea that I would be the sole breadwinner in our marriage. Instead of taking care of his responsibilities to the family, he decided he wanted to pursue his "dream" of playing semi-pro football. If you know me at all, you know I am the kind of person who does not want to hold anyone back from their dreams. Deep

down, I still felt Arnold was a decent person and that he would responsibly take it upon himself to balance his job and his passions. He had played football in college but had never pursued it because he dropped out. But with his newfound enthusiasm for the sport, he started going to practice three nights a week which was great for him, but kept him away from home quite a bit more than was good for our small growing family. And his practices kept getting later and later in the evening, making me suspicious of exactly what he was doing with his time. I finally decided to take a look-see for myself. My Mom and I would go to watch him practice, just so I could put any misgivings I had to rest.

Arnold had no idea that Mom and I were coming to his practice. We parked in a dark secluded area where he couldn't see our car. Just as I looked over at the bleachers, I saw a beautiful blonde girl making eye contact with my husband as he practiced on the field. That was bad enough, but afterwards, he actually had the nerve to walk side by side with her to her car, his arm encircling her waist. He not only opened the car door for her, but got in on the passenger side as well. Both of us in shock, my Mom and I followed hard on her tail towards her house.

With my hand shaking as I picked up my cell-phone, I called Arnold and asked him when practice would be over. He curtly replied, "It will be another hour," and hung up just as abruptly. Mom and I sat there by the side of the street for another hour as the two of them did whatever they were doing. He came out of her house, the pretty little blonde

trailing right behind him. She stood on tiptoes, longingly kissing my husband goodbye. Then he got astride his motor-cycle, gave the throttle a spin and rode off into the sunset! I was absolutely devastated!

Fuming mad, when he got home I angrily confronted him on what I had seen. He flatly denied everything, at least until I told him my Mom had seen it all, too. Realizing he had been caught in the act, he turned on his manipulative charm, begging me for forgiveness. Playing on my emotions and with me being pregnant and wanting my marriage to work, I gave him the benefit of the doubt. But that would only be on one condition — that he quit the semi-pro football team immedi-ately and find a job, which he agreed to do.

I put Arnold's act of unfaithfulness behind me as we prepared for having our first child together. Four months later our beautiful Amanda Lynn was born. She weighed only 7 lbs. and had striking blue eyes and light-colored hair. What a little angel! I was so excited; God had given us this tiny precious jewel! And to my delight, Arnold came to the hospital for a little while saying he couldn't stay long because he had to get back home to watch my son. Jason told his Nanny (my Mom) that he had actually been left home alone that evening because Arnold decided to go out partying that night.

When I returned home from the hospital my neighbors (wives of Arnold's friends) came over to see how Amanda and I were doing. In conversation I was inadvertently informed that Arnold had been seen partying while I was in the hospi-tal having his child. To avoid confrontation, I did not address him directly about the incident; I knew that, like before, he would just deny the whole thing.

In spite of the fact that Amanda was our first child together, Arnold never really had any intentions of helping me with her. He didn't offer to change her diaper and would never get up during her feeding at night, even though I was exhausted and could have used some help. I would even ask him to hold her so I could fix dinner, but he always managed to have an excuse for everything. I thank God for my son Jason, who has always had such a good heart, and loved his little sister and was glad to help in any way he could.

Being a young boy, Jason had desires to do boyish activities. Because Arnold had been a state champion wrestler in high school, he wanted Jason to enroll in the wrestling program in elementary school. With Arnold's help, at the young age of eight years old, Jason became quite an outstanding wrestler. But Arnold was very hard on him. Before a match Arnold would force Jason to pull his body weight to a lower level. This consisted of Jason not eating or drinking all day, which I noticed would affect Jason's energy level and was not good for his health. I did not agree with this, and Arnold and I constantly argued about it. As a result of Arnold's misguided training advice, Jason was not able to finish several matches because he was so weak. Arnold would then become angry, and yell at and humiliate Jason in front of his team members. I finally had to step in and start regularly feeding Jason healthy portions and drinks behind Arnold's back. Jason was then able to win several national titles.

CHAPTER FIVE

New Beginnings

Arnold impatiently looked for a job for three months. Finally, unable to find one, he saw an ad in a magazine in bold type, "Looking for a cable crew in Albuquerque, New Mexico." He immediately called the company and made a bid. Within days he received a call back from them informing him that he got the job. He anxiously contacted ten of his former cable buddies asking them if they would like to work for him. They all replied, "yes." This was the start of our new cable construction business.

The pain... Before Arnold left for Albuquerque, I found out I was pregnant again. In my blissfully naïve state, I thought he would be happy with the news. Instead, he got angry and said that the timing was all wrong. He actually gave me an ultimatum, threatening my life if I did not have an abortion. And he made sure that I followed through by taking me to the clinic the very next day to have the procedure done. This was the most **painful** situation I have ever dealt with in my life, to think that my own husband would want to abort our child.

The following day, with me still recovering from the procedure, a caravan of trucks came to the house, picked up Arnold, and headed to Albuquerque. For seven months these ten guys lived in a two-bedroom apartment, trying to make ends meet as they got the new company off the ground.

Meanwhile, back in Tulsa, I was trying my best to keep our family life stable, raising our two kids alone, as usual. Arnold and I saw each other only four times in the seven month period that he and the cable guys were in Albuquerque. Then Arnold abruptly informed me by phone that his new company had been hired to work in Augusta, Georgia for a two year cable contract. Realizing how much he missed us, he wanted the family to be with him. But because of what had transpired before he left, I was unsure if I even wanted to go with him.

Reluctantly, I once again fell for his manipulative charm. He asked me to quit my job after ten years and cash in my profit-sharing so we'd have money for moving expenses and to hold us over until he got paid. I told him there was only "one condition in which I would quit my job, and that would be if I would have control of budgeting the money and be the secretary for the company." His reply, "Consider it done."

When I told my family and friends they could not believe that I was actually going forward with this plan of sorts. But I did put our house up for rent, and we soon were moving our little family to Augusta, GA. There we found a beautiful two story house to rent and a great church to worship in that the whole family enjoyed. Finally, for the first time since our second year of marriage I felt like we were a family again.

CHAPTER SIX

Living the Good Life

After we were settled in Augusta, I had to quit taking birth control because it was affecting the circulation in my legs, causing blood clots. Two months later I found out I was pregnant with Summer. After having had the previous abortion, I was petrified as to how to tell Arnold. But I was hopeful because we were going to church, thinking he would be excited about the news. By this time, our finances were strong and our relationship was the best it had ever been. But, before I told Arnold the news, I prayed to the Lord for Arnold's acceptance of the baby. It seemed like he had matured since the last incident. To my delight, when I finally told him, he did give me his acceptance. On my birthday, August 2nd, Summer Dawn was born, weighing in at a healthy 9 lbs, with jet black hair and clear blue eyes. She was the best birthday present a Mom could ever wish for.

During this period of time, a lot of wonderful things were happening in our lives. We had all three children baptized and dedicated to the church. And with our contract almost coming to a close, we were pleasantly surprised that we had won a dance contest on the radio. Out of five hundred couples we were chosen to two-step and swing dance at an upcoming Reba McEntire concert. It was so cool!!! Reba, like us, was from a small town in Oklahoma and we felt so comfortable working with everyone in the production company. Our prizes included a limousine ride to the concert, front row seats and backstage passes. When we performed our dance to the Oklahoma Swing we received a standing ovation. Reba is a very genuine and sweet lady; and we were blessed to not only have met her, but to also be a part of her concert. I believe everyone should have a wonderful experience like this once in their lives.

Arnold's next contract brought us to a beautiful area of Virginia Beach. We made our home in a very nice rental not far from the beach. We had wonderful neighbors who were pilots in the Air Force. Always living in a nice neighborhood and nice house, God always provided for my family. Each time we would move, I would say this prayer: *With God's help, I can do all things.*

Move to Jacksonville, Florida... We finished our six month contract in Virginia Beach and then were on our way to Jacksonville, Florida, which turned out to be a very interesting place to live. One downfall of this trip was that the cable crew guys had to work at night making it very rough. And

Arnold was not happy with the way the company handled their business.

By this time, we had a substantial amount of money in savings. Since Arnold wasn't happy at his present job and since there wasn't another job to go to, the family agreed to move back to Coweta, Oklahoma in time for school to start. We bought a house next to his old friend from high school who had been a professional football player and was now retired. Arnold got a cable contract in Tulsa, and everything seemed to be going great.

After we had moved in, a very nice lady left a note on my door to help clean our house. In order to give my family all the time they needed, I hired her to clean my house every Friday, which turned out to be quite a while, as we lived in that home for four years.

As we settled into our life there, Jason, Amanda and Summer got involved in every sport and activity there was available. Jason loved wrestling. Amanda took singing, dance and piano lessons. She was also a cheerleader and played on the basketball team. Summer became a gymnast and took singing, dance and acting lessons from the Musical Theatre Company. I also got involved in many activities, including the PTA, being a Homeroom Mom, Cheerleading Sponsor and a secretary for our Cable business. But Arnold was never around to help me with my busy schedule. Instead, he would spend time with the guys from work when he should have been home helping me with his daughters' needs. And he never seemed to care; all the responsibilities of family life were left on my shoulders. This included taking my girls to school, running errands, attending meetings, taking them to lessons after school, cooking dinner and cleaning house. But my life was very fulfilling. My daughters performed in every contest; and seeing them achieve their goals was very rewarding for me. My girls would always excel as straight A students because their homework was a number one priority. The teacher would often ask me, "How do you do it all?" I would always reply, *"GOD first, family second; balance and have your priorities in line."*

Life was good. Our business was going strong; we were a happy family and I was so proud of my kids. We were growing out of our other house, so Arnold and I decided to build my new "dream" house, Victorian style, inside and out. We designed it ourselves, everything from the ground up. The inside consisted of a marble staircase, and had a stained glass window with a cherub blowing bubbles above the Jacuzzi in the Master Bedroom. There was a cat walk in the entry way and a massive five foot chandelier hanging from the ceiling. We had four bedrooms with huge walk-in closets and four bathrooms. Our sink in the guest bathroom was hand painted.

We found the right builder and a perfect piece of land, eight acres on the edge of town thus beginning a new adventure in our lives. For me, all I could think was "Wow!" Being able to pick out every item for the home, from flooring to paint to appliances and lighting fixtures was overwhelming and exciting at the same time.

CHAPTER SEVEN

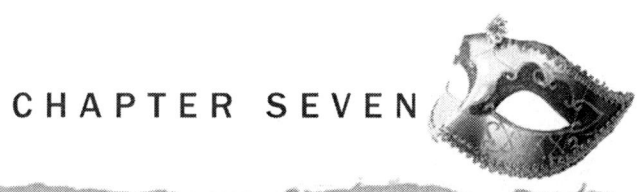

Bad Timing

When our 4000 square foot house was just about three-quarter's complete, Arnold decided to go on his annual four-day hunting trip with his buddies. I was knee-deep in getting all the last minute items for the house ordered, but still had to take care of all my other household responsibilities, which included Amanda competing in a talent contest and Summer a gymnastic meet. I had hoped Arnold would choose not to go on his trip with all the other things we had going on, but he did, anyway. And his phone was conveniently not on, as usual.

Monday night... Arnold was supposed to be returning from his hunting trip when I got a phone call from the alarm company. Apparently, the alarm in our warehouse had gone off accidentally, tripped by Arnold's buddies who were supposed to be on the hunting trip with him. Their story to

me was that they were putting the trailer back in the ware-house when they accidentally set off the alarm. Within ten minutes of them having talked to me, I received a phone call from Arnold, telling me he would be home in a couple of hours. His excuse for his delay was that he was pulling the trailer and it was raining very hard. I played along with him on the phone; but as soon as our call was done, I jumped into my car and drove to the warehouse, to see for myself why he was lying. As my heart pounded, I drove at breakneck speed, close to a hundred miles an hour, making the thirty minute drive in only fifteen minutes. Arriving so suddenly, my brother in-law and three of his friends tried to cover up Arnold's lie, but they were flustered as to what to say to me. I could see from the items they were pulling out of their trucks that they really did go hunting. So while I stood in front of the guys I called Arnold and confronted him, wanting to know the truth about where he really had gone for the weekend. He stuttered, knowing he was caught, and confessed to me, "I have been with a young twenty-two year old girl in New Orleans." My heart sank; it was absolutely the worst timing! I stood there, reeling, not knowing which way to turn. As the conversation continued, the only thing I could think was *if I divorce him right now we probably won't get the loan for our house.*

Thinking back on that day, I should have left him right then and there, and the ending of this story would have been so very different. But that is not the choice I made. While we were still on the phone, Arnold begged me to stay with him.

In an attempt to hold on to me he said, "While I was with this twenty-two year old I realized she wasn't worth leaving my family for."

At that moment I wish there had been some way I could have talked him into going to a marriage counselor; perhaps then things might have been different. But in my desperation, I didn't have anyone to turn to, or confide in, and I didn't tell anyone because my girls were still in school and I didn't want anyone to know the pain I was experiencing. All I felt was humiliation and betrayal. My heart fell to my feet. I had really thought that I would be married for life, and yet, my life was crumbling around me. I felt absolutely helpless. I prayed to the Lord for words of hope and encouragement. Here's what came to me:

Let Go...Let God
When you're searching for truth
and you can't find your way
when people don't hear what you're trying to say
and the answers won't come to the things that you pray
~it's time to let go and let God...

All of my very being was wrapped up in my children and my husband and our life together. And yet, I couldn't talk to a soul about what was really going on.

Months went by and we finally finished our dream house. What was supposed to be a joyous time turned out to be very disturbing. I wondered what to do and tried to trust again.

But the nightmare would not go away. It kept on haunting me. I found "her" phone number on his telephone bills again. I finally got enough guts to just call her. Trying to understand why this was happening to me again, I asked her pointed questions. She admitted to me on the phone, "I am a stripper in a club in Oklahoma City." It seemed she was totally unaware that he had a family, and continued saying, "All I am interested in is his money." Now it was all making sense. Arnold always wanted to be the big shot boss to all his employees. In an attempt to impress his buddies, he would pay for their lap dances and drinks all night long.

Apparently, Arnold and his crew had been staying a week at a time in a motel right across the street from the stripper club. Since Oklahoma City is two hours away from Tulsa, he would only come home on weekends. In spite of his little excursions to the strip joint, he would call me every night and tell me how much he appreciated and loved me; and how he couldn't wait to get home for the weekend. He would often say, "You are such a good wife and mother."

As soon as I finished my conversation with the "other woman" I felt very uneasy. For the life of me, I couldn't grasp why he continued to do this. Heartbroken and restless, I lay my head down in attempt to get some needed sleep. My restless mind finally drifted off into a dreamlike state where I saw several women dancing around my husband. Startled, I awoke, aware of the presence of an angel standing at the foot of my bed. "You must go to Oklahoma City," she said, and then quickly disappeared.

Now, the word angel means "messenger." Some theologians say that angels are God's love, manifested. They are usually depicted with wings to distinguish them from human beings. Yet, we are told, angels are among us in ways we may not understand. I decided to heed this heavenly messenger's advice.

So, the following evening, I made the long trip to Oklahoma City without any hesitation. When I arrived at my destination, I didn't want anyone to see my car so I parked behind a restaurant two doors down from the motel where Arnold was staying. I walked to the front of the restaurant and seeing a taxi parked there, I approached the driver's window and explained my sticky situation to the cabby. Since I didn't want to be seen, I had him take me to the motel and strip club. He was such a compassionate man, and insisted on staying with me the entire time. Around eleven p.m. Arnold called my phone (like clock-work) to say his goodnight. Not surprisingly, no sooner had I hung up when I saw him and the other guys walk out of the back of the motel and straight into the front door of the strip club. Seeing this, my nerves began to shake, upset and afraid all at once.

Whenever I start feeling like this, it helps me to think on the scriptures. This is what came to my mind and gave me peace in the situation:

Cast all your anxiety on Him...because he cares for you. [1 Peter 5:7]

The next day, I confronted Arnold. Once again, he whined in his same "poor me" way and denied any wrongdoing. In my mind, this last stunt was bad enough, but what made it even worse was that he had taken my son along for the ride. (Months later, I would find out from Jason that Arnold had threatened him not to tell me.) I was unforgiving; it was the last straw. I had lost all respect for him and any of the warm feelings I had were absolutely gone. The only affection I had left for him was because he was the father of my children. That was it.

CHAPTER EIGHT

A Word for Jason

What should have been a normal Thanksgiving family dinner turned out to be very disturbing for my poor son, Jason. During the course of the day I noticed that he was not his usual outgoing self, but very jittery and quiet at our usually festive table. After dinner we all decided to see a movie, but Jason didn't want to go with us. Upon our return we found Jason in his bedroom, his eyes puffy from crying. I couldn't help but ask, "Honey, why are you so upset?" He looked up at me, his eyes filled with tears, and said, "Mom, I have been up for seven long days and feel like I am ready to die." "But why were you up for so many days and feel like you are dying?" I needed an explanation to understand. In a flood of emotion, he blurted out, "Mom, I've been hanging around with the wrong people and taking a drug which keeps me up at night. It curbs my appetite and so I haven't felt like eating at all. And sometimes it makes me act differently, makes me mean to people around me. I knew this wasn't me, but I felt so helpless and couldn't quit on my own. So I cried out for help...and God spoke to me." This is what God showed Jason from His Word:

Now the Lord has said to Abraham "Get out of your country, from your family and from your father's house, to a land that I will show you. 2 I will make you a great nation; I will bless you and make your name great; and you shall be a blessing. 3 I will bless those who bless you, and I will curse him who curses you; and in you all the families of the earth will be blessed." [Genesis 12:1-3]

Jason continued explaining, this time reading Psalm 138:7 to me:

Though I walk in the midst of trouble, you preserve my life, you stretch out your hand against the wrath of my enemies and your right hand delivers me.

I then said "Jason, I believe in this scripture from Proverb 22:6":

"Train a child in the way he should go and when he is old he will not turn from it."

I gave my son a big hug reassuring him that I loved him and was so proud he had turned his life around back to God. Jason then went to sleep peacefully. Today, ten years later, Jason is living his life in a way that demonstrates to all the skeptical non-believers that he did hear from God that day and that God really did change his life.

CHAPTER NINE

Confronting the Fear

Arnold's deceit was finally catching up with him. He had lost control and his manipulative ways were not working on me anymore. The more he found himself losing control of our relationship, the angrier he became...

One particular night, I brought up his last affair while my daughter happened to be in the room. I guess I didn't care any more. Embarrassed, you could see the rage in his face as he said to my daughter "Go up to your room — now." After she left, he physically picked me up and slammed me down on the kitchen counter. Wrapping his fingers around my vocal cords, cutting off my windpipe, all I could do was pray, *"God help me!"* As he choked me, he raged, "Don't you ever say anything about my affairs in front of my daughters or you will never breathe again." I grasped for air as he released his deadly grip around my throat. Running into the bathroom, I dialed "911," staying in my room until the police arrived. My girls, not knowing what had transpired, ran downstairs screaming "Please don't put my Dad in jail." Only thinking of them kept me from pressing charges. Deep down I knew for my own sanity that I had absolutely no choice but to get out of this marriage.

More abuse... One night after a birthday dinner with my friend Kim we had a last toast with a glass of wine at the restaurant. As a result, I got home around midnight, later than I anticipated. Thinking everyone was asleep, I lay down on my pillow, only to suddenly feel the pressure of his foot on my head. It was so forceful; it pushed me two feet up against the wall. Then he jumped out of bed and kicked me for a second time. He grabbed fistfuls of my hair and slammed my head hard against the floor. The pain was excruciating, and I just lay there crying hysterically to God for help. "This will show you not to come home late," he said angrily, and got back into bed. Emotionally exhausted I fell asleep on the cold floor. The next morning I awoke, sore, bruised and headachy. Looking into the bathroom mirror, I could count the bruises all over my body. I had to think fast, as I had made plans to go to a PTA meeting that morning. Not wanting anyone to know, most of all my daughters, I covered myself up as best as I could. To avoid the shame I felt inside I whispered to myself *"Let go...let God. This is only temporary... this too shall pass."*

More abuse and control... while coming up my long winding driveway one day after work, I noticed a burnt area in front of our garage. Curious, I got out of the car to see what it

was: a bunch of burnt clothing hangers in a pile. I went inside, up the stairs and straight to my closet, and saw that half of my clothes were missing. "Arnold," I questioned. "What the heck happened?" "This," he said, pointing a vindictive finger at me, "is your punishment for wearing revealing clothes." Shocked at his bizarre behavior, I held it together as best as I could while making dinner. He later went outside the garage and cleaned up the evidence before the kids got home to see it.

More abuse.... on this particular day, I thought Arnold was going straight home from work...but once again, he had other plans. I had gone to the local gym to work out. During my routine, I asked a young trainer to show me how to properly use one of the weight machines. He was very nice and stopped what he was doing to help me. I finished my workout, and about an hour later left the gym. Curiously, Arnold wasn't there, when I got home, but about thirty minutes later he walked in the door with a frightening look on his face. His hair was disheveled, his shirt ripped, and he had blood on his hand and a scratch on his face. So I had to ask him "What happened to you?" His reply was frightening. "I took care of that young punk at the gym. He was trying to make a pass at you when I drove by the window." "He was just doing his job!" I said, exasperated. I turned to leave so I could see what kind of condition Arnold had left that poor, beat-up trainer in. As I did, Arnold lunged at my arm, turning me upside down, pulling my phone out of my hand and ripping my fingernail off, which bled profusely. I had to wrap and hold it in a hand towel to try and stop the bleeding. As I ran to my car to leave, he beat me to the garage, unhooking the door opener so I couldn't get my car out, and get away from him. I felt like a prisoner in my own home, and didn't understand why I was going through such constant pain. I sat in my car for hours, afraid to enter the house until the kids got home. As I sat in the car, I prayed:

Let go of the bad and the good will appear,
Trust in the knowledge that He's always near,
That answers and choices are always more clear
When you can let go and let God.
Just lift up your hands and surrender your heart,
Tell Him your worries and He'll do His part.
Let go of the past and your future will start,
When you finally let go and let God.

Finally, fear left me and I knew I had to get a divorce no matter what the consequences might be.

At times, life's path
seems filled with things
that make the going rough,
And we wish there were
a smoother road,
for we feel we've had enough...

But, if we pause a moment
and remember Who's in charge,
The hills that loom ahead of us
no longer seem so large,
And every rock before us,
when we know we're not alone,
Becomes, not just a stumbling block,
but a stepping stone.

Emily Matthews

Summer '95

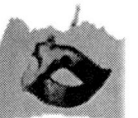

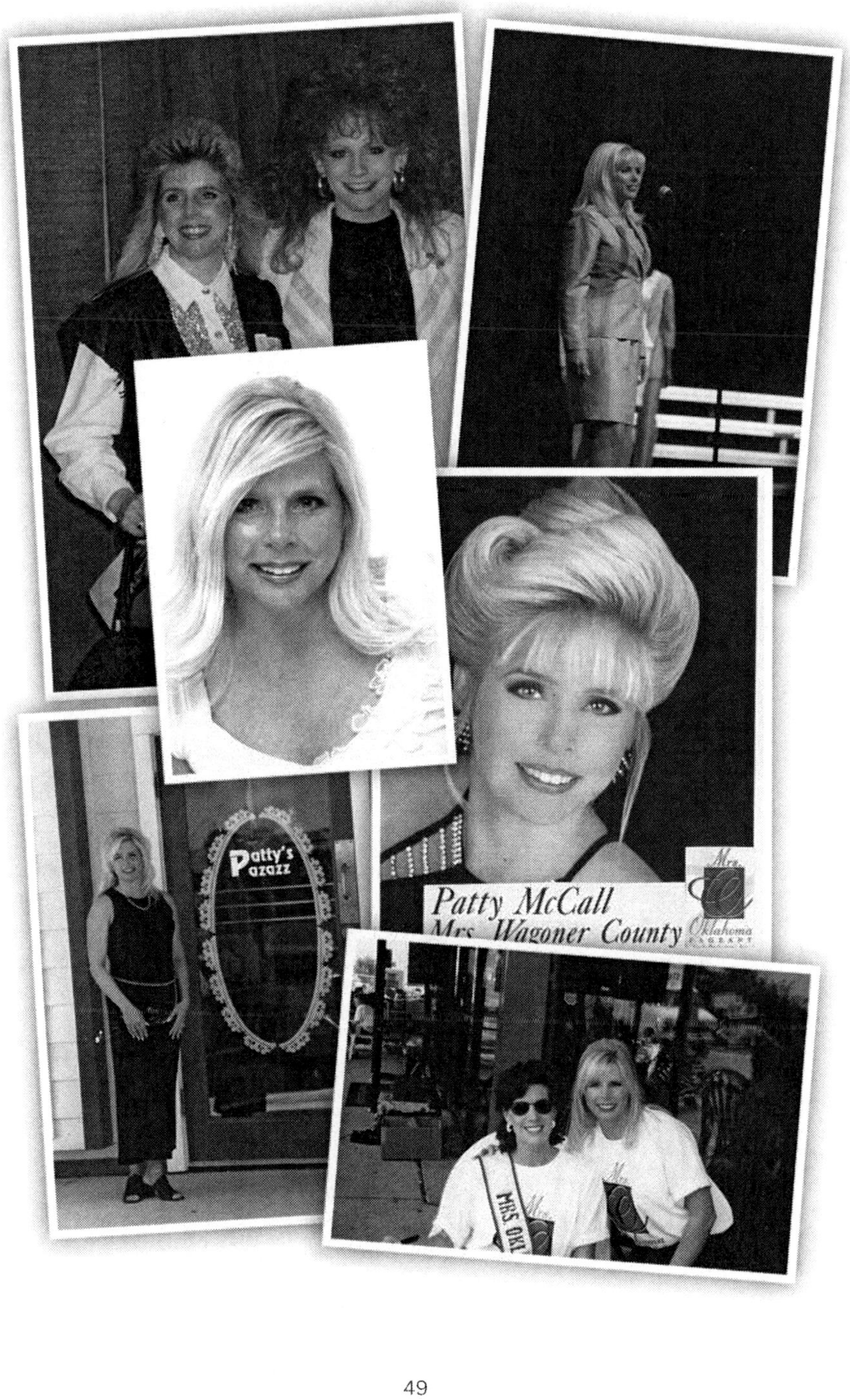
Patty's
Pazazz
Patty McCall
Mrs. Wagoner County

This was just a sample of Patty's photo album which
included her son Jason, his wife Angel and her grandson
Izick, her daughter's Amanda and Summer.
Her Mom Irene and various photos of herself
which includes her guy, Romeo.

CHAPTER TEN

Losing Control

If I was to secure my independence from Arnold, I knew I had to take active steps in that direction. I left the cable business as Arnold's secretary, but wasn't exactly sure what my next move should be. What direction should I go in to find my self-worth? I would say this prayer everyday:

Trust in the Lord with all your heart, and lean not on your own understanding; and all your ways acknowledge Him, and he shall direct your paths. [Proverbs 3:5-6 NKJV]

I prayed about the situation and felt the Lord guide me.

Soul searching and guidance in the right direction... In one month's time, I contacted friends from high school, started having weekly lunches with other moms, and opened my own clothing boutique. I started traveling to the "Dallas Apparel Mart" once a month, to purchase clothing for my business with my beautician friend. My new boutique was opening up endless opportunities for me: fashion shows for the prom, tux rentals for weddings. I even became a Board Member for Miss Oklahoma and Director for the "Little Miss Fall Festival." My daughters started working at the store after school, which was a big help to me and taught them responsibility. My Mom also got involved. She loved to fill in for me which gave me time to attend my daughters' functions. Even my Friday house cleaning lady joined in and became my right arm at the store. It was great the way we worked together. She picked up where I left off; always anticipating what I was thinking.

During this time, my positive-thinking peers encouraged me to compete in the Mrs. Oklahoma Pageant. I reigned as Mrs. Wagoner County. I thought it might be fun to see what it was like to be on the other side. It also gave me a chance to express the importance of "The Six Pillars of Character," which are: **Respect, Responsibility, Caring, Trustworthiness, Fairness** and **Citizenship.** The Character Counts Platform I represented gave me the opportunity to speak at various types of organizations and elementary schools.

During this time Arnold thought I was becoming way too independent, and could feel me slipping away from his tight grip. Out of desperation he begged me to renew our wedding vows, grasping at anything to make my feelings for him return. I was at a loss for words and couldn't believe he had the audacity to even ask me. I could tell by his choice of words he was in denial of the past. A part of me desperately wanted to be able to say to him, "Yes, it will be alright again," but the other part of me knew that with Arnold there was always a calculated motive behind his actions. But, if I didn't go through with it I would always wonder what could have been. In spite of all our problems, I still hoped that there could be a new beginning for us and my children.

CHAPTER ELEVEN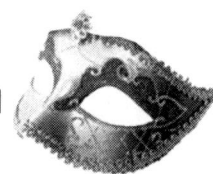

Entering the Twilight Zone

The unknown... Two weeks later, the wedding vow renewal ceremony took place in our house. The guests consisted of immediate family and a few close friends.

With a limited budget and the help and support of my dear friend, Rachel, it all came together. The dresses came from my boutique; Rachel acted as my photographer, hairdresser and seamstress. My daughter Amanda played the piano. Jason and Summer stood up for us in the ceremony. The overall appearance looked absolutely stunning in everyone's eyes.

When the music started playing the "Wedding Song" scenes of my abuse at Arnold's hands flashed before my eyes. I felt like I was in the **twilight zone,** in a trance-like state as I walked down the stairs toward the preacher and Arnold. I stood there in disbelief, and it all happened so fast, before I knew it the ceremony was over and people were hugging me. Arnold, wanting reassurance, asked me after the ceremony, "Did you like how the preacher presented the vows?" I couldn't even respond. Everything was a big blur to me. Without answering, I changed the subject and proceeded to walk away from him, mingling with the crowd.

CHAPTER TWELVE

Fighting for Life

One day out of the blue... Arnold suggested we "Take out more life insurance on the two of us." He said that the cost for the spouse would not make a " big" difference, and that we also had a lot more equipment which needed to be covered." The conversation somehow gave me a funny feeling in my stomach. Since I had lost complete trust in my marriage I knew he was probably up to something evil. In his usual sly way, he once again convinced me to go forward with it, mentioning it was a good idea so our daughters would also be taken care of if something happened to "us."

About six months later... I found myself getting sick to my stomach. Just before I would go to work in the morning Arnold would insist on bringing me a cup of coffee, acting like he was doing me a kindly favor. This went on for a few weeks, and every day, half way to work I would have to pull over to heave out of the car door. It felt like I was pregnant, but a year earlier I had gotten a hysterectomy so I knew that was impossible.

But his evil plan wasn't working quickly enough... one particular evening, Arnold knew the kids were spending the night with their friends. Knowing spaghetti is my favorite meal and that I would eat every bit of it, Arnold decided to serve me a delicious plate. When it was ready, he called me from the bedroom, saying "Oh, Patty! Your favorite dinner is waiting for you on the table." I came immediately.

Two hours later... Every ten minutes I had to run to the bathroom sick to my stomach, spitting up blood.

As time went on... I progressively got worse. Dehydrated and weak, I had developed sharp pains in my stomach, so intense that I would scream doubled over in excruciating pain. I begged Arnold to please take me to the emergency room, to which he dryly responded, "Oh, you'll be okay, get some sleep." Realizing he was not the least concerned, I called my Mother from my bedroom. Shaking with urgency in my voice, I gasped, "Mom I am so sick. I need to go to the hospital and Arnold won't take me." "Honey is that the pig you are talking about or your husband?" She was trying to make light of the conversation. "I will be right there." As she came up the driveway Arnold asked me sternly, "Did you call your Mom?" "You don't understand, Arnold, I feel like I am going to die," was my weak response. Distractedly, he said, "I have to go to the bathroom." He quickly proceeded to the bathroom shutting the door. My Mom held on to my arm walking me to the car. As she opened the passenger door she said with concern on her face, "My sweet Patty, can you lift your legs to get in the car?" "Barely," I dazedly replied. She placed a bucket on my lap in case I got sick during the drive.

We arrived at the hospital's emergency entrance. Mom quickly filled out the necessary paperwork, and the nurse's assistant took me to a room for observation. The nurse asked "What have you been eating and drinking?" "I have been sick for a couple of weeks after drinking my morning coffee," I said, "A few hours ago I had spaghetti for dinner. An hour later I became ill to my stomach." The nurse showed concern in her face, and immediately took my vital signs and ran the necessary tests. While all this was going on I continually ran to the bathroom. The tests returned showing I had rat poison in my system. They did more tests, after which she gave me something to drink to flush out the poison. I started feeling a little better. The nurse said to me, "I believe the rat poison was in your food and in your coffee. Do you know anyone who would want to harm you or how it got in your food? Do you have rat poison at your house?" I replied, "Yes, in my kitchen cabinet underneath the sink. We used it for a rat that was in my garage from the field." The nurse advised me, "Do not drink or eat anything your husband fixes for you. And bring your coffee to the laboratory to be tested." "Thank you for your concern and help," I said to the nurse, "I will definitely take your advice." They released me from the hospital and I went home to my Mom's house to try and get some rest.

He didn't stop there... Arnold knew the rat poisoning scheme had failed.

His next plan was... a trip to Colorado where we always took the girls with us snowmobiling. Since Arnold couldn't keep secrets to himself he told his best friend from school the only way he was going to pay off his million dollar debt was to kill me, receive the full amount of life insurance (one million dollars) and take the kids.

His plan was... to take me to Colorado, have a snow mobile accident, causing me to go over the mountain...then leave me there for dead where no one would find me. Well, luckily for me, his best friend couldn't keep this information to himself. He told his wife that evening.

The next day... she came to my boutique and begged me not to go to Colorado, explaining why. I looked at her in shock, realizing Arnold would go to any extreme to kill me. I asked my friend, "Why is he so desperate?" Her response suddenly made it all make sense. "He wants the life insurance money." The puzzle was slowly coming together. But I still hadn't realized what the **largest missing piece** was.

That evening, I told Arnold I was not going to Colorado with him because my Mom was sick and I had to take care of her. He was angry with me, knowing his evil plan was failing for the second time.

CHAPTER THIRTEEN

Paying the Piper

The missing piece... About the time I was trying to prove Arnold's plan to kill me, the police came to the warehouse to arrest him...*through the Lord always being there for me.*

Arnold was arrested for thirty counts of fraud. He had made false invoices to a loan shark company which was fronting him money on subcontracted jobs. He owed them almost a million dollars. Thank God I didn't know anything he was doing. My signatures were not on the checks anymore. He was giving me some money for household expenses and any extra money I needed for me and my daughters I earned through my clothing boutique.

Arnold was released on bail after three days in jail. During this time he became very mean, irritable and bitter, and at times talked of suicide. Since his name was completely banned from the cable TV business, he decided that the only way he could pay back the debt to the courts was to go in business with Bill, who owned the shopping center. As time went on Arnold still could not make ends meet. He would come to my store and sit there all day trying to figure out how much I was making so I could help pay back his debt. While I was away Arnold put a small recording device on my business phone taping all my conversations.

CHAPTER FOURTEEN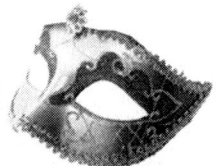

Reaping the Whirlwind

One Afternoon... For no apparent reason he wanted to take me out to dinner. He acted like it was a "special" day; that he wanted to tell me some good news. When I got in the car I had to know, "What is the good news?" But he would not tell me, stalling by saying "I'll let you know after dinner." When we left the restaurant around 9:30 pm I noticed he was driving towards a different path than usual. The paved road we were on suddenly turned into a **dark dirt road.** He pulled the truck over to the side of the road saying to me, "This is what you have been waiting for all night." He took a tape out of his pocket and put it into the tape player. The recorder played a conversation between me and my Mom earlier that morning. He heard me confiding in my Mom, talking about financial pressures, and Arnold's manipulative ways etc. At the end of the conversation I confided with her that I had to get a divorce before I went insane. As I heard the recording, I shook inside, not knowing what was up Arnold's sleeve.

All I could do was pray. These thoughts from God came to my mind: *"God is my all; I know no fear, since God and love and truth are here." There was nothing for me to fear when I realized that I brought the presence of God with me wherever I went. Instead of letting fearful thoughts consume me, I let the light of God shine out from me during this difficult time, creating a shield of loving energy that extended outward to comfort and protect me and others from fearful thoughts. "You, O Lord, are a shield around me." Psalm 3:3*

He became violent... shaking me, grabbing my vocal cords so hard that I couldn't breathe, screaming at me in a deep dark voice, "You will never divorce me. And if you try to leave me you will leave with 'only' the clothes on your back, **if I let you live tonight.**" I was trying to get my breath back sitting there in shock. I sat silently all the way back home.

CHAPTER FIFTEEN

Finding Love

One evening... I was at the mall with my daughter, when Arnold called me in a very mean, stern voice, "Get home and cook my dinner, you don't need to be getting her anything." I hung my phone up, told myself with a prayer of strength... *I am not going to be controlled anymore by this evil person... I have strength with the Lord by my side.* I felt inner **peace** knowing that I had received divine guidance...an inner knowing of what was right for me — when all uncertainty had subsided and I felt at **peace** with my decision. **Peace** is the key element I seek when I need to know whether I am on the right path.

I left the mall, went out with my friend to a country bar to put **the pain** away and enjoy myself for the rest of the evening. I was just standing by the bathroom when this really cute guy asked me, "Why aren't you dancing?" Without hesitating I spontaneously replied "Because you haven't asked me yet." He grabbed my hand and swept me off to the dance floor. We danced for four beautiful hours. It was invigorating feeling like a kid again with butterflies in my stomach and happiness in my heart. Temporarily I felt no **pain.** My partner and I both knew in our hearts that we didn't want to leave each other's side. So, we closed the club down. The few of us left decided it would be nice to go to breakfast. "Romeo" and I had such a terrific conversation with each other. I felt perfectly at ease, in fact, he made me laugh until my sides hurt. One of Romeo's friends laughed, saying to me, "I don't know what you have, but Romeo never dances with the same girl more than one song." When Romeo's friend was paying the bill, Romeo looked at me and said, "You, darlin' are going with me. You are the only woman that has stopped me in my tracks."

And **it did not stop there...** We went to a hotel. It was such a romantic, intense and dynamic feeling that I had never experienced before. We were inseparable, staying together for two weeks. I called my girls and Mom the next day, telling them I was alright. I told them on the phone I needed time away to think about my life.

I looked at this moment as a once in a lifetime dream which I hoped would never end. I didn't understand why this person was in my life, but I didn't second guess it. *I let go...let God.*

CHAPTER SIXTEEN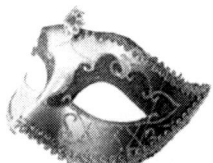

Returning to Reality

Reality set in... Coming to terms that my dream was ending, I thought...

I needed to go home to my teen daughters. This was the first time in my life I had been away from them that long.

Romeo had an opportunity to work and stay with one of his Air Force buddies in Missouri. As hard as it was to leave each other we both knew this was the best thing for now. The day we parted it was a very sorrowful moment. We knew in our hearts we were going to see each other again. Romeo said to me, "Call me when you get a divorce."

When I arrived home it was so great to see my girls. I had missed them so much. But I had nothing to say to their father, even though he tried to interrogate me and find out where I had been. But, this time it didn't work. He saw in my facial expressions that I lost all feelings for him and was numb. I kissed the girls good night and told them I loved them. I continued to the guest bedroom to go to sleep.

CHAPTER SEVENTEEN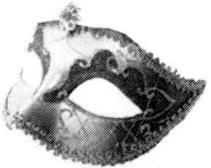

Escaping from Hell

Arnold had to go back to the courts several times during the year, each time bringing at least five thousand dollars towards his million dollar debt. He had promised to bring the courts more money at his last visit, but did not keep his word, so the judge unexpectedly sentenced him to prison that very day.

The next day... early that morning in big bold letters across the front page of the local newspaper it said that Arnold *was indicted for thirty counts of fraud, sentencing him to thirty years in prison.* Within minutes of me picking up the paper my phone was ringing off the hook.

Living in a small town is like living in a fishbowl; everyone tries to stick their nose in your business. When a major incident happens it's like a feeding frenzy around the town.

This was equivalent to reading an article in the "National Enquirer." As I read the article, it struck me that this was my chance to finally escape from the hell which I endured all these years.

I immediately started divorce proceedings, all the while trying to figure out how my daughters and I were going to financially survive on our own. I looked in his briefcase one day and saw a stack of bills thrown in there. As I flipped through the papers, it terrified me to realize we were two or three months behind on all our bills, including the mortgage payment. In desperation I put up an "Everything Must Go" sign in front of the house.

The next day... my home was flooded with people buying my valuables, furniture etc. It was during this time that Arnold received the divorce papers I had filed. His friend told him I was selling everything in the house. His lawyer informed him, if he signed the divorce papers he could stop me from selling everything because he was entitled to half.

CHAPTER EIGHTEEN

Sorting through Chaos

Chaos was happening all around me... I could not get Romeo out of my mind. We stayed in contact on the phone. I talked to Romeo a couple of weeks before mentioning I had filed for divorce. The following week Romeo called me to check on the situation. I told him my house was in a shambles and I needed a real man's help. I described to him how bad it was. The lawn was waist deep, the pool was green with algae and the garage was filthy.

I did not have any money to pay someone to clean up the mess, so I asked Romeo if he could come to my rescue. Romeo told me on the phone, that he was ready to leave Missouri and come to Oklahoma to be with me. He said, "It has been too long... I miss you very much." The timing was right. He was there for me in a couple of days cleaning the pool, mowing the eight acres and cleaning out the garage. When my girls found out exactly who Romeo was they were furious at me, and to add fuel to the fire, Arnold was writing letters to them, bad-mouthing me. My girls felt sorry for their Dad in prison. They did not want me to leave him because I had never told them about the abuse I had endured at their Dad's hands.

CHAPTER NINETEEN

Empty Promises

Arnold's lawyer and the company he had defrauded persuaded the judge to let him out on one stipulation: that he would pay the court back monthly through a new cable contract he was supposed to be getting.

Promises... Promises... Promises.

The next day... I thought I saw a ghost when Arnold walked into my boutique. For a man I had known intimately for so many years, I did not recognize him at all, as his head was clean-shaven. As usual, he started by lying to me, saying, "I came to get my briefcase." But the real truth was that he wanted to interrogate me; I could see the look in his conniving eyes.

The Pain... The hardest decision of my life was to move away from my daughters. At the time, it was my only answer, and yet it was a heartbreaking decision, one I had to make to keep what sanity I had left. I had "no more fight" left in me. Every time I would try to explain my side of the story they would gang up against me, and there was no getting through to them; Arnold had done a very effective job of brainwashing the girls. During his prison stay, Arnold had so played on the girls' emotions and sympathy that I knew it was a losing battle. In his own manipulative way, he would make them feel guilty and sorry for him. The girls told me they wanted to stay at the house with their Dad, even though I knew it was only a matter of time before the mortgage company was going to foreclose on what had been my "dream house."

CHAPTER TWENTY

Humiliating Circumstances

I had no choice but to move to an apartment in Tulsa, Oklahoma, thirty minutes away from my store in Coweta. Amanda left for college attending Texas A&M in Galveston, Texas, while Summer was still living in our house with her Dad. Sadly, she did not know where I was living for quite a while, as I was not comfortable with anyone knowing where I was. I felt like I was alone living in a fish bowl.

Arnold had grown up in this small town with his family, and he tried to turn the whole town against me and make everyone feel sorry for him. He would get their sympathy by saying, "Can you believe she left me for a young boyfriend while I was still in prison?"

But the people in town were not aware of my side of the story. The abuse I endured while married to him was always kept **within** me. I never told anyone. They only heard his side of the story. Arnold was able to manipulate their minds to such an extent that they would look down on me, thinking me an insensitive person that had lost her mind and was on drugs. Even though I was no longer under his control, I was still haunted by our past due bills, and as might have been expected, a couple of months later bill collectors served me papers at my business. I found out there were notes from his business that my signature appeared on.

The Pain... I had no choice but to close the doors to my boutique and file bankruptcy. Even my passion, the only thing I had loved and worked so hard for was being taken away from me. I said a prayer for the Lord's strength to help me stay strong, keep my chin up and not look back. This was only a temporary setback. A door closes so a better one can open.

CHAPTER TWENTY ONE

A Second Chance

I was wrong again... changing jobs did not stop Arnold from making my life miserable and stalking me.

I found a job at a Doubletree Hotel working as a hostess in their very elegant restaurant. But when I would get off work Arnold would be in the parking lot waiting for me, his motive only to follow me and find out where I lived. Thinking logically and trying not to be scared, I would go back to the front of the hotel and wait until he left. I wasn't going to deal with his scare tactics and games anymore, so I filed a restraining order against him. Of course, this made him furious. Arnold can't stand it if someone is one step ahead of him. In his world, he has to have the last laugh.

It didn't stop him... Even though we were three months into our divorce, Arnold was still determined to make my life miserable. He was very vindictive since I had sold the Jaguar and bought a Corvette. Any time of the day or night I had to constantly look over my shoulder to see if anyone was following me. Finally I came to the realization that I had to leave.

The Pain... I didn't want to leave my daughter, Summer. But she wanted to stay in Oklahoma, and there was nothing I could do about it.

Six Months later... the night before we were leaving for California we put all our belongings in a twenty-four foot U-haul truck. When we got up in the morning we noticed the tires on the car hauler were flat. Romeo and I didn't waste time figuring out why this happened. We called the U-haul company to come and fix the tires. I didn't want anything distracting Romeo's focus. But someone must have found out we were leaving. While we were preparing to go, I started getting an eerie feeling that we were being watched. I said to myself, "I have to get out of here."

On our way to California... Romeo and I felt someone had set us up. We were about an hour away when the cops pulled us over for the first time. The second time we were in Texas. Both times they searched the U-haul and checked Romeo's personal belongings, not finding anything. They proceeded to go through our furniture, throwing pieces off the back of the truck breaking each one. The cops walked up to the truck saying, "You are free to go now."

We felt someone was still up to no good... our truck broke down in New Mexico. We stayed overnight in a ghost town where the U-haul service station was. Apparently the

mechanics at the service station didn't do a good job, as we broke down again in Arizona. They were finally forced to bring us a new truck to which we had to switch all of our belongings.

Four days later... we finally arrived in California. This had been the trip from hell.

Here I thought I was starting with a clean slate, but I had to jump over a "new" hurdle. I found out some startling news about my new man. Thankfully, I knew because of the hell I had gone through with my marriage, any **obstacles** that came my way would only serve to make me **stronger** and **wiser.**

I found out from Romeo he was a very crazy and daring guy, but I just didn't know how crazy. Just before I met him, he had been released from the hospital, having been in a coma as the result of being shot and stabbed. He had sustained these injuries during a drug deal that went bad, and would not have survived if it wasn't for the intervention of his best friend who found him for dead. After this critical incident, Romeo turned his life around, realizing God has given him a "second chance" on life. I felt with God's guidance and my support Romeo would be able to stay on a "straight and narrow" path way.

Back in Oklahoma, when I knew I was going to leave for California I had spoken to a guy who sold ads for me when I had my boutique. Since he was originally from California and moving back there, he mentioned to me that we could share a place with him temporarily. I had sent him money for rent and a deposit to move in.

The old saying is "You don't know someone until you live with them." I thought he was a friend, we found out differently...

When we arrived in California I contacted him. We moved all our belongings into his place hoping we could stay for awhile.

But no, we were wrong... He told us he was a body builder. In order to keep up his body-building physique he had to take steroids every day. I noticed, that there were days on and off he would come home acting spacey; the steroids causing him to have major mood swings.

One day... Romeo left his flip flops in the middle of the living room floor, not thinking this guy would have a fit over something so ridiculous. Well, this apparently was a day when his mood swing kicked in and it didn't take a lot for his temper to rise out of control. He spotted the flip flops on the floor, turned to Romeo and threatened to throw him over the balcony. He then locked us out of the apartment since it was in his name. I had to get the police to get our belongings out of there and a moving company to move us. This nightmare happened all in one day. Since we didn't have a lot of money we ended up staying on the beach in Romeo's truck. This went on for an entire week.

Finally, we found a nice apartment in Santa Clarita, and slowly began to realize that the cost of living in California was way more expensive than Oklahoma. Since I couldn't keep up the payments on my Corvette and also pay for rent, I was forced to sell my beautiful car for dirt cheap. And

Romeo's truck wasn't reliable; it broke down shortly after I got rid of my car, so, we had to rent a car for a few weeks. With all this happening, we knew that making a life here was going to be a huge **challenge.** All we did was work to live, but we were determined to make California our "home sweet home" together.

CHAPTER TWENTY TWO

Last Ditch Attempts

The Fear... Just when I thought Romeo and I were going to have peace in California a desperate phone call came. It was the mother of my daughter Summer's best friend telling me confidential information. She related to me with panic in her voice "Patty, Arnold is going to take Summer out of the country. He got her a passport. If he does not come up with eight hundred thousand dollars ($800,000) within three days they are going to put him back in prison for the thirty years. Since Arnold has come to the realization he won't have the money, he has planned to get on a plane before his court time. You and I know he has no intentions of coming back to the US. If he comes back there will be a million dollar bond on him." She continued to say, "You have to stop him or you'll never see your daughter again!" With relief, I said to her, "I can't thank you enough for sharing this with me. I am leaving tonight." I prayed to the Lord for guidance, and I felt Him tell me, *"Go now, there is no time to waste."*

Since I was not financially able to purchase an airline ticket, Romeo and I knew the only alternative we had was for us to drive back to Oklahoma. We grabbed some belongings and headed down the highway. From California it would take twenty four hours driving non-stop. It felt like the longest trip ever! My **fear** was so intense. I alternately panicked and then prayed the whole way, knowing I was against a race for time.

Driving through Texas... I desperately wanted to call my attorney for help, but I still owed him money from the divorce I knew he wouldn't talk to me. My only option was to call legal aid and explain my situation. They were very helpful putting me on the docket first thing the next morning. Immediately a woman lawyer called me back expressing her concern and wanting to help me. "In order for me to under-stand how I can assist you, I need to have some details," she said. As I tried to calm down by catching my breath I explained, "My ex-husband and I have joint custody of my fifteen-year-old daughter . . . ," and continued filling her in on all the necessary details. She ended the conversation reassur-ing me, "I will be at the courts to represent you."

The next day... we arrived in Coweta, Oklahoma. Upon approaching my old house I saw Summer getting into Arnold's cousin's van. When his cousin saw my car she immediately took off, acting like I was coming to kidnap my own daughter. After chasing her for awhile, she must have realized we were not going to give up that easy, so she pulled over to the side of

the road. Screaming at me, she said, "You are not taking Summer with you." I yelled back, "Don't you know he is going to take her out of the country tomorrow. I won't let this happen!" She pushed me down on the ground, and I fell into a ditch. Then she jumped into her van and left the scene. Picking myself up, I ran to the car, saying "Romeo, let's go; we need to call the cops!" I called the police station explaining the full details of the situation. Within minutes I heard sirens in front of us. As I put my hand outside the window directing them where to go, they stopped their van. Through the squad car speakers they told everyone, "Get out of the vehicle." They informed Arnold's cousin, "There will be a court date tomorrow, and you need to bring Summer and her passport with you," adding, "If you don't abide by the law you will go to jail."

At the courthouse... the judge spoke to everyone separately in his chambers, listening to each story. Summer and Arnold's cousin were firmly told by the judge, "Your passport is frozen until you are nineteen years old. You are not going out of the country with your Dad. He apparently brainwashed you. Thinking you will be living in an Embassy house on the beach and that you'll have plenty of money is a lie." She was very upset with the decision.

Throughout all this turmoil, the legal aid lawyer was always by my side as well as my mother. None of the positive things would have been possible without them supporting me.

A decision was finally made for Summer to stay with Arnold's cousin under certain law-abiding rules until other arrangements could be made. Since Summer was used to living very well, I did not want to take her out of her comfort zone, and I knew Arnold's cousin had received several thousands dollars from his grandmother's will; they were living in a new house and had plenty of money to take care of Summer. His cousin expressed to the judge, "My husband and I want Summer to stay with us temporarily."

The Pain... I was so sad when I heard Arnold's cousin say what she did. Deep in my heart this wasn't what I wanted at all for my daughter. I wanted her with me in California. But she was only 15 and didn't want to leave her friends at school. I would have moved back immediately from California, if she had wanted me to, but I think she was afraid my financial situation wouldn't be enough for her. Well at least this is what she had been convinced of even though I knew I would do whatever it took to provide for her. I am a survivor and a very hard worker. Having poured my whole life into my kids, it killed me to have to leave her. I tried not to feel guilty for the mess our lives had become. None of us could understand, but she was so adamant at this point to stay, and I couldn't convince her to come with me. And to think, I was the one who had raised her to be so independent. At one point, Summer turned to me and said, "Mom go on and we will see each other as much as possible." But I could hear in her voice that she was still hurt and angry.

My worst fear was over... while we were all hashing out the details in court, Arnold had actually taken off in a plane and left the United States.

CHAPTER TWENTY THREE

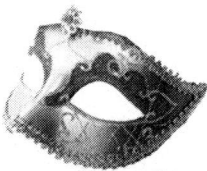

Follow Your Dreams

As a Mom my dreams and peace of mind are knowing that my kids are following their dreams and living their lives moving in the right direction.

Summer is now attending TU University majoring in marketing and is a co-ed cheerleader.

Amanda graduated May 2008 after putting herself through four years of college. She graduated with a Bachelor's in Science and a Degree in Marine Transportation.

Jason prayed to meet the right girl to marry, and along came his lovely wife. "Angel." They attend church together and are actively involved in youth ministry. Every week Jason ministers at the local prison, and when the opportunity arises Jason is quick to share his testimony in order to help others to know Christ. He believes that our body is the temple of God as the Word says. He often enters body-building contests, and gives God the glory. Jason and Angel had my first grandbaby in August 2008. What a joy... the greatest blessing of all.

Life in Hollywood has finally started making a turn for the better. Networking and marketing is the key for success in the entertainment business. With persistence and hard work Patty has began succeeding her life long dream. For the past four years Patty has been surrounded by actors, producers and directors.

Starting as a background performer she met very influential people in the industry. One day in the late afternoon Patty was taking a stroll down Sunset Boulevard when her attention turned towards a beautiful stylish Bentley car, which was parked on the street. The owner of the vehicle was putting bags in the trunk of the car. Patty said to the gentlemen, "I like your car." He replied with a smile on his face, "Are you an actress?" I laughed saying, "isn't everyone here in Hollywood?" He replied with a chuckle in his voice, "No really, I am a Producer and have a part for you in a sci-fi film."

He then gestured by giving me a casting director's card. He began to say, "Call her tomorrow." I proceeded to walk away saying thank you to him. The next day I followed-up by calling the casting director. We had a nice conversation on the phone and by the end of the conversation she set up an appointment for me to come in the next day. When I met with her I was immediately cast for a speaking role to play a "trophy wife."

Carmen Bentoncourt, a casting director and a dear friend of mine sent me to an audition for a movie called "Montana Amazon." When I met with the producer at the audition she asked if I was available to meet with the hair and make-up people the next day for a photo shoot for the movie. They cast me for the role of "Kitty." It was a small but intense role. I was Taft Hartley into the SAG Union.

Becoming a producer is definitely the most challenging position in the entertainment business. I have several qualities and past experiences that directed me in this path. Starting at the age of ten in my backyard I produced a circus for the neighborhood. Simply coordinating fashion shows, helping with behind the scenes in theatre and being a production coordinator on commercial and music videos. It all contributed to becoming a film producer.

When I met Lisa Ann and Emperor Frederick Von Seidl in November of 2007 I was asked to be a part of their production team and family. It seemed to be the right choice for me.

Patty and Romeo... Yes, they are still together. Talk about a storm of a relationship. The love they share is so deep it keeps them strong through the massive storms. They are living in Los Angeles, traveling and sharing the same interest in work, such as hosting and producing. Riding their bikes and enjoying the beach are their favorite interests together.

The pursuit of happiness is everything... Believe in yourself, follow your **dreams** and everything will fall into place. This is what I have experienced since I have been in California.

Spiritual Guidance And Peace For Women...

This book is meant to inspire women and give them **hope,** **strength, encouragement** *and* **self-worth.**

Spiritual Recipe to Overcome and Move On

You **overcome** *by:*

> *Having faith in God, and believing in yourself,*
>
> *Treating yourself and others with dignity and respect,*
>
> *Taking the good, asking God for strength to conquer the bad, and letting peace rule in your heart.*
>
> *Then, in all that comes your way, you will prevail.*

You **move on** *by:*

> *Having* **confidence** *in yourself*
>
> *Living in* **healthy** *surroundings;*
>
> *Getting* **support** *from others in your community*
>
> *Taking an interest in something that you love and have a* **passion** *for,*
>
> *Getting involved in helping others*
>
> *Freedom comes the moment you see the truth.*

Domestic Violence Help Information
For Public Awareness and Crisis

Websites and Crisis Line:

Haven Hills

Website: www.havenhills.org

Crisis line: (818) 887-6589

Outside of Los Angeles: 1(800) 799-7233

Peace Over Violence

Website: www.peaceoverviolence.org

24 Hour Hot Line:

(626) 793-3385; (310) 392-8381; (213) 626-3393

W.I.S.H (Women In Safe Homes)

Website: www.oklahomabedandbreakfast.net

Direct Line: (918) 683-3900

Crisis Line: (918) 682-7878

About the Author

Patty McCall is a native of Oklahoma. She worked for a financial institution for ten years as a supervisor in customer service and marketing. A loving mom of three, Patty devoted much of her time as a Home Room Mom, PTA member, and Cheerleading sponsor.

As the owner of a clothing boutique she became involved with the Chamber of Commerce, which led to coordinating fashion shows, becoming a Director for the Miss Fall Festival, a National Talent Judge, and a Board Member for the Miss Oklahoma Pageant. She also participated in the Mrs. Oklahoma Pageant and reigned as Mrs. Wagoner County.

Patty and her daughters were naturals in all aspects of the film industry; from print to commercials and theatre to modeling. This natural ability led her to a new career as the owner of McCall Talent Agency located in Muskogee, Oklahoma. In 2004, Patty relocated to California to become an Assistant Director for the Young Actors Camp. She is a teacher and production coordinator for Joey Travolta's Short Film Camp for Children and an acting coach for children at the Dedicated Talent Agency. She has also worked as a TV host for "Hollywood Weekly" and "Blonde Talk Now."

Currently, Patty is involved with the organization, "Milphworld" which stands for Mothers, In Life, Passion and Health. She continues to follow her passion for performing with various supporting roles in television series and films, such as "Montana Amazon," being released in 2009.

Patty is currently a Co-Producer on a comedy/musical film which is in pre-production. The movie based on this book, *Unmasking the Pain Within,* will start pre-production in 2009.

CPSIA information can be obtained at www.ICGtesting.com
263904BV00005B/3/P